INVESTIGATING GHOSTS IN CEMETERIES

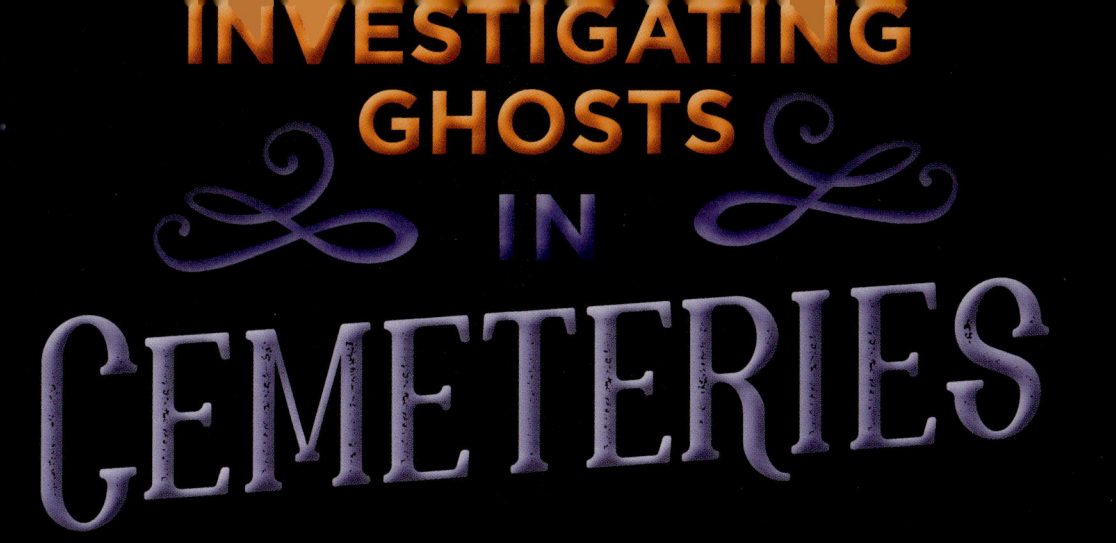

Matilda Snowden

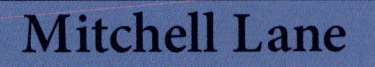

Mitchell Lane
PUBLISHERS

mitchelllane.com

2001 SW 31st Avenue
Hallandale, FL 33009

Copyright © 2021 by Mitchell Lane Publishers. All rights reserved. No part of this book may be reproduced without written permission from the publisher. Printed and bound in the United States of America.

First Edition, 2021.
Author: Matilda Snowden
Designer: Ed Morgan
Editor: Joyce Markovics

Series: Investigating Ghosts!
Title: Investigating Ghosts in Cemeteries / by Matilda Snowden

Hallandale, FL : Mitchell Lane Publishers, [2021]

Library bound ISBN: 978-1-68020-616-6
eBook ISBN: 978-1-68020-630-2

PHOTO CREDITS: Design Elements, freepik.com, cover: Shutterstock, p. 5 Shutterstock, p. 6 Sandy Millar on Unsplash, p. 7 freepik.com, p. 8 freepik.com, p. 9 Karl Thomas Moore CC-BY-SA-4.0, p. 10 Joonas Sild on Unsplash, p. 11 Photo by Joel Overbeck on Unsplash, p. 13 Alamy, pp. 14-15 Cobra97 CC-BY-SA-3.0, p. 17 Cobra97 CC-BY-SA-3.0, Shutterstock, pp. 18-19 Cobra97 CC-BY-SA-3.0, p. 19 STARPICZ / Splash News/Newscom, p. 21, 22 Infrogmation of New Orleans CC-BY-SA-4.0, public domain, p. 23 LuckyLouie CC-BY-SA-3.0-migrated, pp. 25, 27 Dancing with Ghosts CC-BY-2.0, p 26 freepik.com

CONTENTS

1 Graveyard Ghosts　　　　　　　　　4

2 Union Cemetery　　　　　　　　　　8

3 Bachelor's Grove Cemetery　　　　14

4 St. Louis Cemetery No. 1　　　　　20

5 Agua Mansa Pioneer Cemetery　　24

Ghost-Hunting Tools　　　　　　　28
Find Out More　　　　　　　　　　29
Works Consulted　　　　　　　　　30
Glossary　　　　　　　　　　　　　31
Index　　　　　　　　　　　　　　32
About the Author　　　　　　　　　32

Words in **bold** can be found in the Glossary.

CHAPTER ONE

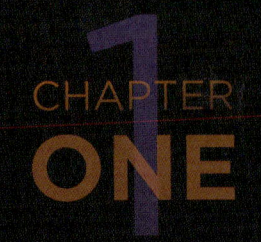

GRAVEYARD GHOSTS

The moon glows above an old cemetery. A ghost hunter crouches behind a mossy gravestone holding a video camera. The air is still and silent except for chirping crickets. The sky darkens as a large cloud swallows up the moon. Just then, the ghost hunter hears a strange moaning noise. She presses the *record* button on the camera. Suddenly, the camera stops working. The sound turns into an ear-splitting wail. A greenish-yellow mist forms before her eyes. It creeps over the stones. Then, as quickly as it appeared, the mist disappears into the night sky.

Cemeteries are where dead people are laid to rest. But it seems that some of the dead have come back to haunt these usually peaceful places. At cemeteries across the country, people have claimed to see ghosts and other eerie things. What explains these spooky sightings? Do ghosts really exist? There is a **devoted** group of people who want to find out. These ghost hunters, also known as **paranormal** investigators, gather **evidence** to prove that ghosts are real.

Turn the page to read spine-tingling stories about reportedly haunted cemeteries. And follow teams of paranormal investigators who seek to uncover the truth about ghosts.

INTERESTING FACT

What are ghosts? They're thought to be the spirits of dead people that appear to the living. There are said to be many different kinds of ghosts. One Japanese type is called *buruburu*. It's believed the *buruburu* attach themselves to people's spines, making them shiver in fear.

CHAPTER TWO

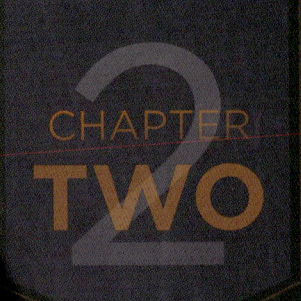

Union Cemetery

Easton, Connecticut

It was a cool, spring evening in Union Cemetery in Easton, Connecticut. Brothers Tony and Ryan Vosper were playing among the headstones when they saw an odd, bright light. It was unlike anything they had ever seen. Even stranger, from inside the light, they spotted the form of a woman. "We stopped playing and just stared," remembers Ryan. Then the glowing figure began to float!

Tony and Ryan saw that the figure was wearing an old-fashioned wedding dress and **veil**. As they looked closer, they saw little "dark forms" surrounding her. Shaken with fear, the brothers ran to their house. They told their parents about what they had seen. Tony and Ryan were sure they had seen a ghost.

INTERESTING FACT

The Union Cemetery dates back to the 1700s. It sits beside an old church. Some ghost hunters have said that the graveyard is the most haunted place in the United States.

The ghost spotted by Tony and Ryan Vosper is known as the White Lady. Years before the Vosper brothers saw her, a drifter had his own eerie encounter at Union Cemetery one night. As he rested in the grass, a glowing female figure appeared. She wore a white dress, and small, dark shapes encircled her. Then she vanished.

The White Lady also appeared to a man whose wife had recently died. One evening, he visited his wife's grave at the cemetery. Filled with sadness, he fell to his knees. Just then, he saw the White Lady watching him. Then she softly said:

"I wish my husband would have loved me as much as you love your wife." Seconds later, the apparition was gone. These and other encounters have made Union Cemetery a popular place for paranormal investigations.

Two of the most famous paranormal investigators, Ed and Lorraine Warren, went to Union Cemetery to search for the White Lady. The Warrens set up a video camera in hopes of recording her. For days, nothing happened. Then, one night at 2:30 a.m., a glow appeared. It took the form of a woman in a flowing white gown. And she wasn't alone. As in the other sightings, there were dark forms around her. Strangely, the Warrens couldn't see the figure in the camera's viewfinder, even though she was clearly in front of them. Then, *poof*, the White Lady was gone.

The Warrens worried that they hadn't captured the ghost on camera. But, when they viewed the tape, they were filled with delight. The footage showed the glowing image of a woman in a long dress.

Ed and Lorraine Warren

INTERESTING FACT

During their long career, the Warrens have investigated more than 10,000 hauntings, using video cameras and other equipment to perform their work. They've collected lots of evidence, which they say proves that ghosts are real.

CHAPTER
THREE
3

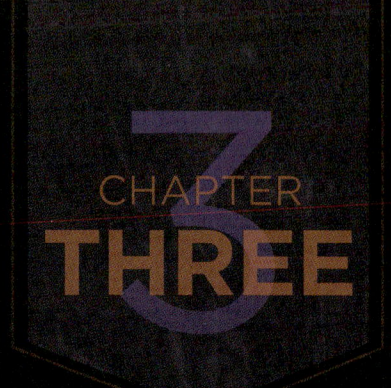

Bachelor's Grove Cemetery

Midlothian, Illinois

Outside of Chicago is a quiet, wooded, and very haunted cemetery called Bachelor's Grove. Hundreds of spooky sightings have been reported there. The paranormal activity ranges from **phantom** farmers to dancing **orbs**. No one knows why the cemetery is a hotspot for things not of this world. But ghost hunters are on the case.

One of the most well-known ghost stories takes place in the 1970s. Two forest rangers were **patrolling** the area when they saw something strange in a pond. Out of the water appeared an old man driving a horse and plow. The man, dressed in worn overalls, held tightly to the horse's **reins**. The rangers were stunned.

INTERESTING FACT

In 1991, Judy Huff-Felz of the Ghost Research Society captured a famous image of a ghostly woman sitting on a gravestone in the cemetery. To this day, no one has been able to explain the ghostly presence in the photograph.

Paranormal investigators think this story might help explain the haunting. According to a legend, a farmer lived near the cemetery many years ago. He was plowing his fields one day when his horse got spooked. The animal ran into the pond, dragging the farmer with it. He became tangled in the reins. The heavy plow quickly sank into the water, pulling the horse and farmer to their deaths.

In addition to the phantom farmer, unexplained lights appear in the cemetery. They're often colorful streaks of red or blue that dart across the sky. At times, the orbs grow and shrink. Baseball-sized balls of blue light have even been known to chase people. For decades, ghost hunters including Zak Bagans, have tried to capture the spooky lights on film.

17

One night in 2012, Zak Bagans and his ghost-hunting team went to Bachelor's Grove. He asked police officers to guard the grounds to prevent anyone from tampering with the investigation. As Zak and his crew walked around, they saw "a ball of light." At first, Zak thought it was a police officer's flashlight. Then he saw the orb hovering and darting in and out of the woods. And, shockingly, it began following the team! It was no flashlight. Luckily, Zak's crew caught some of the glowing orbs on camera.

What explains the lights and ghostly activity? Some paranormal investigators think that Bachelor's Grove was built on an ancient burial ground filled with restless spirits. Others believe that rocks deep below the cemetery produce magnetic fields. These powerful fields may affect people's vision, causing them to see orbs and other strange things. What's the truth? The mystery remains.

Ghost hunter Zak Bagans

INTERESTING FACT

Zak Bagans is on a TV show called *Ghost Adventures*. He and other ghost hunters try to debunk claims of paranormal activity. They say it's as important as finding evidence of a ghost.

CHAPTER FOUR

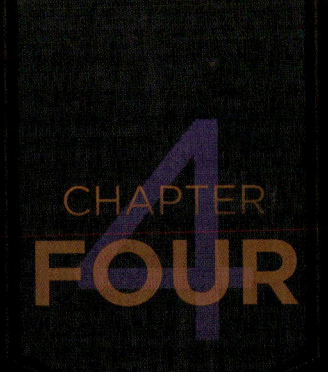

ST. LOUIS CEMETERY NO. 1

New Orleans, Louisiana

With more than 100,000 graves, St. Louis Cemetery No. 1 is called a city of the dead. Dating to 1789, it's New Orleans's oldest cemetery. It's known for its winding walkways and aboveground stone tombs. It's also famous for ghosts—and the people who hunt them.

One tomb in the cemetery is visited more than all the others. It belongs to Marie Laveau, also called the Voodoo Queen.

When she was alive, Marie was known as a powerful Voodoo priestess. Today, curious visitors flock to her grave. However, they're often met with a fright. Years ago, it's said that one man was joking about Marie. That's when an unseen hand slapped him across the face. When he whipped around, no one was there.

INTERESTING FACT

Marie Laveau lived from 1801 to 1881. She was known for her *tignon*, a cloth headdress with seven knots.

21

Some people believe Marie's spirit appears as a black cat with red eyes or as a huge snake. Marie was supposedly buried with her pet snake "Zombi." It's said that Zombi followed a woman who spit on Marie's grave. Later, as the woman slept, Zombi appeared in her bed! With all these stories, one has to wonder: Is Marie's spirit at rest?

Dozens of ghost hunters have investigated Marie's tomb. One used a special audio recorder. He was hoping to capture an EVP. EVPs, or Electronic Voice **Phenomena**, are what paranormal investigators believe are "spirit voices." The ghost hunter recorded an EVP of a woman moaning. Was it Marie once again making herself known?

Some ghost hunters use handheld infrared thermometers to detect temperature changes supposedly caused by ghosts.

INTERESTING FACT

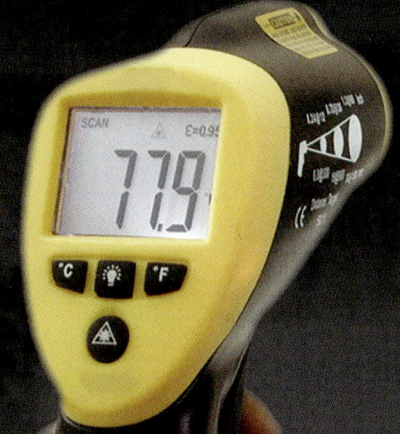

In a typical investigation, ghost hunters spend hours looking for paranormal activity. They use dozens of tools, such as cameras, recorders, thermal imaging tools to capture hot or cold spots, and special meters that pick up energy fields. Then they sift through all the data for evidence of ghosts.

CHAPTER FIVE

Agua Mansa Pioneer Cemetery

Colton, California

When Eric Bermumen was a kid, his parents drove past Agua Mansa Pioneer Cemetery one night. Eric looked out the window expecting to see a few headstones. But, instead, he saw something terrifying. "I saw a guy walking a dog and it looked like the guy had no head," remembers Eric.

Dating to 1854, Agua Mansa has stories scary enough to make even the bravest among us shudder. From headless ghosts to floating phantoms, there is plenty to investigate. Is there any truth to the scary sightings at Agua Mansa?

INTERESTING FACT

In the 1980s, two dead bodies were found in a pickup truck at Agua Mansa's gates. And in 2004, the cemetery's caretaker took his own life. Some people say that their ghosts can also be found on the cemetery's grounds.

Ghost hunter Paul Groslouis went to Agua Mansa Pioneer Cemetery to search for spirits. He says he saw a female ghost with long, wet hair, floating toward the cemetery's gates. It seems he encountered La Llorona, or the Weeping Woman.

According to one legend, La Llorona drowned her children and herself after her husband betrayed her. Another legend has it that La Llorona's children died when the Santa Ana River flooded in 1862, destroying the village of Agua Mansa. It's likely that no one will ever know why the Weeping Woman haunts Agua Mansa. Beware if you go there in the dead of night.

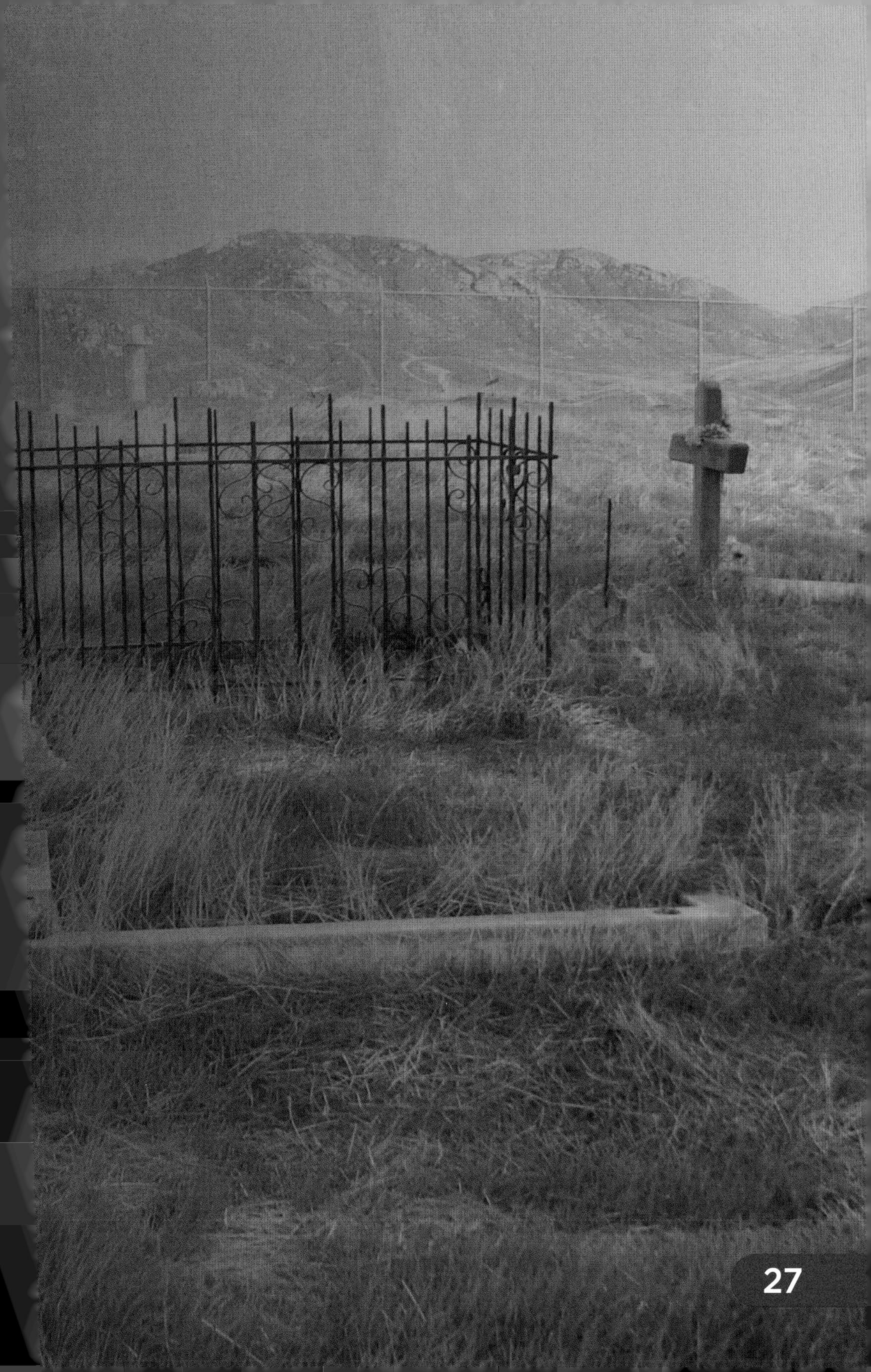

Ghost-Hunting Tools

Here are some basic ghost-hunting tools. Many household items can be used to track and gather evidence of possible ghosts.

- Pen and paper to record your findings
- A flashlight with extra batteries
- A camera with a clean lens. Sometimes, the "orbs" that some people capture on film are actually dust particles on the lens.
- A cell phone to use in case of an emergency and to keep track of time
- A camcorder or digital video recorder to capture images of spirits or any other paranormal activity
- A digital audio recorder to capture ghostly sounds or EVPs
- A digital thermometer to pick up temperature changes

More experienced ghost hunters use thermal imaging tools to locate hot and cold spots, as well as special meters to pick up energy fields. These include EMF (electromagnetic field) and RF (radio frequency) meters.

Find Out More

BOOKS

Allen, Judy. *Ghostly Graveyards*. New York: Bearport Publishing, 2016.

Gardner Walsh, Liza. *Ghost Hunter's Handbook: Supernatural Explorations for Kids*. Lanham, Maryland: Down East Publishing, 2016.

Loh-Hagan, Virginia. *Odd Jobs: Ghost Hunter*. Ann Arbor, Michigan: Cherry Lake Publishing, 2016.

WEBSITES

American Hauntings
https://www.americanhauntingsink.com

American Paranormal Investigations
https://www.ap-investigations.com

The Atlantic Paranormal Society
http://the-atlantic-paranormal-society.com

Ghost Research Society
http://www.ghostresearch.org

Paranormal Inc.
http://www.paranormalincorporated.com

The Parapsychological Association
https://www.parapsych.org

Works Consulted

Dwyer, Jeff. *The Ghost Hunter's Guide to Los Angeles*. Gretna, Louisiana: Pelican Publishing Company, Inc., 2007.

Dwyer, Jeff. *The Ghost Hunter's Guide to New Orleans*. Gretna, Louisiana: Pelican Publishing Company, Inc., 2016.

Newman, Rich. *Ghost Hunting for Beginners: Everything You Need to Know to Get Started*. Woodbury, Minnesota: Llewellyn Publications, 2018.

Taylor, Troy. *The Ghost Hunters Guidebook: The Essential Guide to Investigating Ghosts & Hauntings*. Alton, Illinois: Whitechapel Productions Press, 2004.

Taylor, Troy. *Haunted New Orleans: History & Hauntings of the Crescent City*. Charleston, South Carolina: The History Press, 2010.

Warren, Ed and Lorraine, with Robert David Chase. *Graveyard*. Los Angeles: Graymalkin Media, 2014.

On the Internet

https://www.bachelorsgroveforever.com/about

http://www.ghostresearch.org/sites/bachelors.html

http://ghoula.blogspot.com/2008/03/inland-empire-paranormal-investigators.html

https://www.latimes.com/archives/la-xpm-2004-oct-29-me-cemetery29-story.html

https://nyupress.org/9781479815289/

Glossary

apparition
A ghost or ghostlike image

betrayed
Broke a promise or turned against

debunk
Prove to be untrue

devoted
Very loyal

drifter
A wanderer

encounters
Unexpected meetings

evidence
Information and facts that help prove something

legend
A story from the past that may not be entirely true

magnetic fields
Regions around a magnetic material or a moving electric charge

orbs
Glowing spheres

paranormal
Relating to events not able to be scientifically explained

patrolling
Walking or traveling around an area to protect it or to keep watch on people

phantom
A ghost or spirit

phenomena
Occurrences that one can sense

reins
Straps used to control or guide a horse

spirits
Supernatural beings such as ghosts

tampering
Interfering with something in order to cause damage or make changes

thermal
Relating to heat

vanished
Disappeared

veil
A piece of cloth worn to conceal the face

Voodoo
A religion that includes some traditional African beliefs

Index

Agua Mansa Pioneer Cemetery	24–27	La Llorona	26
apparition	11	Laveau, Marie	20–23
Bachelor's Grove Cemetery	14–19	magnetic fields	18, 28
Bagans, Zak	16, 18–19	Louisiana, New Orleans	20
Bermumen, Eric	24	orbs	14, 16, 18, 28
buruburu	7	paranormal investigators	6, 11–12, 16, 18, 23
California, Colton	24		
Connecticut, Easton	8	phantoms	14, 16, 25
Electronic Voice Phenomena (EVP)	23, 28	spirits	7, 18, 22–23, 26, 28
		St. Louis Cemetery No. 1	20–23
evidence	6, 13, 19, 23, 28	thermal imaging	23, 28
ghost hunters	4, 6, 9, 14, 16, 18, 23, 26, 28	tools, ghost-hunting	23, 28
		Union Cemetery	8–13
gravestones	4, 15	Voodoo	20–21
Groslouis, Paul	26	Warrens, Ed and Lorraine	12–13
Huff-Feltz, Judy	15	White Lady, The	10–12
Illinois, Midlothian	14		

About the Author

Matilda Snowden loves visiting cemeteries and all things old and cobwebby. Her favorite thing about being an author is talking with children about how to tell a spooky story.